For Yasmin Gilders - a special little girl,
and her mum - a special friend   V.P.

For Mum and Dad   D.W.

OXFORD
UNIVERSITY PRESS

Great Clarendon Street, Oxford OX2 6DP

Oxford University Press is a department of the University of Oxford.
It furthers the University's objective of excellence in research, scholarship,
and education by publishing worldwide in

Oxford New York

Auckland Bangkok Buenos Aires Cape Town Chennai
Dar es Salaam Delhi Hong Kong Istanbul Karachi Kolkata
Kuala Lumpur Madrid Melbourne Mexico City Mumbai Nairobi
São Paulo Shanghai Singapore Taipei Tokyo Toronto

with an associated company in Berlin

Oxford is a registered trade mark of Oxford University Press
in the UK and in certain other countries

Text copyright © Vic Parker 2002
Illustrations copyright © David Whittle 2002

The moral rights of the author and artist have been asserted

Database right Oxford University Press (maker)

First published 2002

British Library Cataloguing in Publication Data
Data available

ISBN 0–19–279077-3 (Hardback)
ISBN 0–19–272487-8 (Paperback)

10 9 8 7 6 5 4 3 2 1

Printed in Singapore by Imago

The Yo-Yo King

by Vic Parker

illustrated by David Whittle

OXFORD
UNIVERSITY PRESS

Can you send a yo-yo whizzing down-up-down?
To be a real cool kid, you have to yo-yo in this town.

Everybody's at it - on the street, at home, the park...

We yo-yo before breakfast. We yo-yo after dark.

Mike's even has a brain!

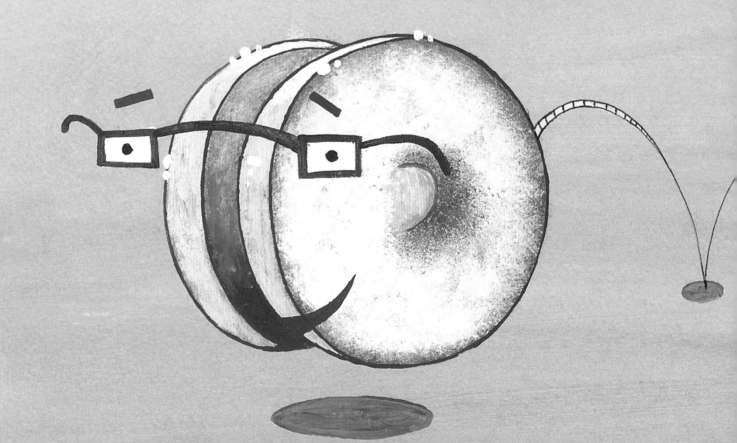

It stops itself and spins...

and then it bounces back again.

wwaaaaaaaag

Marcy's makes a screaming noise
(she says that it's alive).
And Eric says his brother
has got three or four or five!

One day a little kid came up we'd never seen before.
He asked if he could play with us –
W·e·l·l...we weren't so sure.

'What's your name?' we challenged.
'Kareem Hakeem,' he said.
    'Do you want to see me yo-yo?
I bet I knock you dead.'

'Show us then,' said Brian,
(a little sharp I thought).

The kid just shrugged and said, 'Stand back!' and from his pockets brought
- an old wooden yo-yo, rather scratched and small.
It wouldn't flash, or think, or scream - nothing special at all.

We looked at it and giggled.
The kid just looped the string.
He flexed his fingers, raised his hand

and then he did his thing.

It scraped the ground, it touched the sky,

that yo-yo - it could dance and fly!

Sparks whizzed out as it tossed and whirred.
Our heads felt dizzy, our eyes were blurred.

There's nowhere that yo-yo didn't go.
Like lightning it spun to and fro.

Until, quite suddenly, it came to land

still and safe in the
palm of his hand.

Well, now the kids run up and shout
when Kareem and his yo-yo are about.

'How do you do it?' 'Please show us too!'

'We want to yo-yo just like you.'

But they know they'll never be that great even if they live till they're a hundred and eight.

For Kareem Hakeem's the Yo-Yo King!
No one yo-yos anything like him.

Still, if worst came to worst and he lost his knack,
or his yo-yo broke, or his string went snap,
I'll always be glad that in the end,
Kareem Hakeem is my best friend.